For Sidney William
D.W.

For Sophie
C.S.

Fun-to-Read Picture Books have been
grouped into three approximate readability
levels by Bernice Moon, teacher-in-charge,
Ellington Language and Literacy Centre,
Maidenhead, Berkshire. Yellow books
are suitable for beginners; red books
for readers acquiring first fluency; blue
books for more advanced readers.

This book has been assessed as Stage 8
according to *Individualised Reading*, by
Cliff Moon and Norman Ruel, published by
the Reading and Language Information Centre,
University of Reading.

First published 1988 by
Walker Books Ltd
87 Vauxhall Walk
London SE11 5HJ

Text © 1988 David Wood
Illustrations © 1988 Clive Scruton

First printed 1988
Printed and bound by
L.E.G.O., Vicenza, Italy

British Library Cataloguing in Publication Data
Wood, David, *1944 Feb. 21-*
Sidney the monster.–(Fun-to-read picture books)
I. Title II. Scruton, Clive III. Series
823′.914[J] PZ

ISBN 0-7445-0559-3

Written by David Wood
Illustrated by Clive Scruton

WALKER BOOKS
LONDON

There was once a monster called
Sidney. "I'm bored," he said.
"I fancy some frightening."

So he rang a doorbell and hid.

When the lady opened the door…

Sidney jumped out and
poked his tongue out at her.

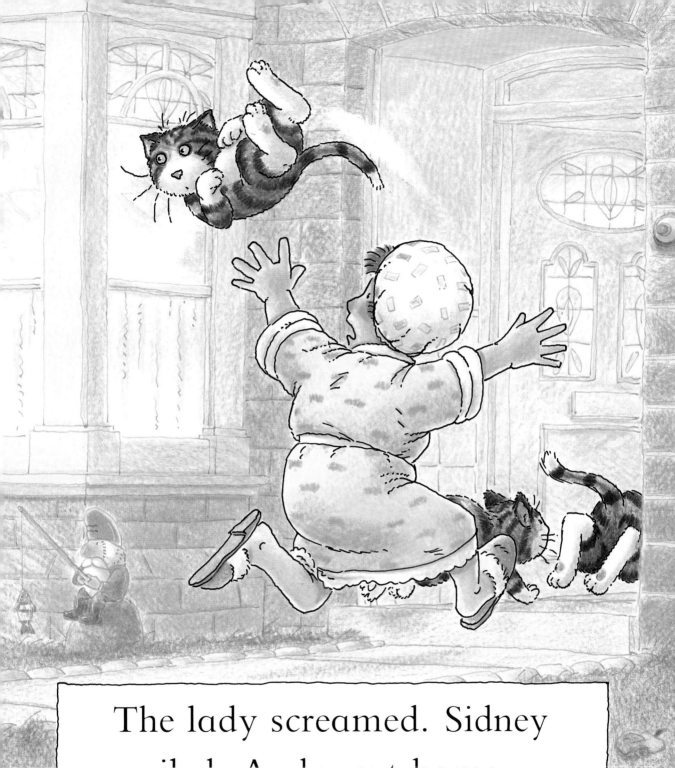

The lady screamed. Sidney smiled. And went home.

"I'm still bored," said Sidney.
"I fancy some more frightening."

So he went to the supermarket and
pretended to be a frozen chicken.

When a customer tried to pick
him up…

Sidney popped up and shouted, "BOO!"

The customer fainted. Sidney
giggled. And went home.

"I'm still bored," said Sidney.
"I'll go frightening again."

So he went to the park and

jumped into the pond with ...

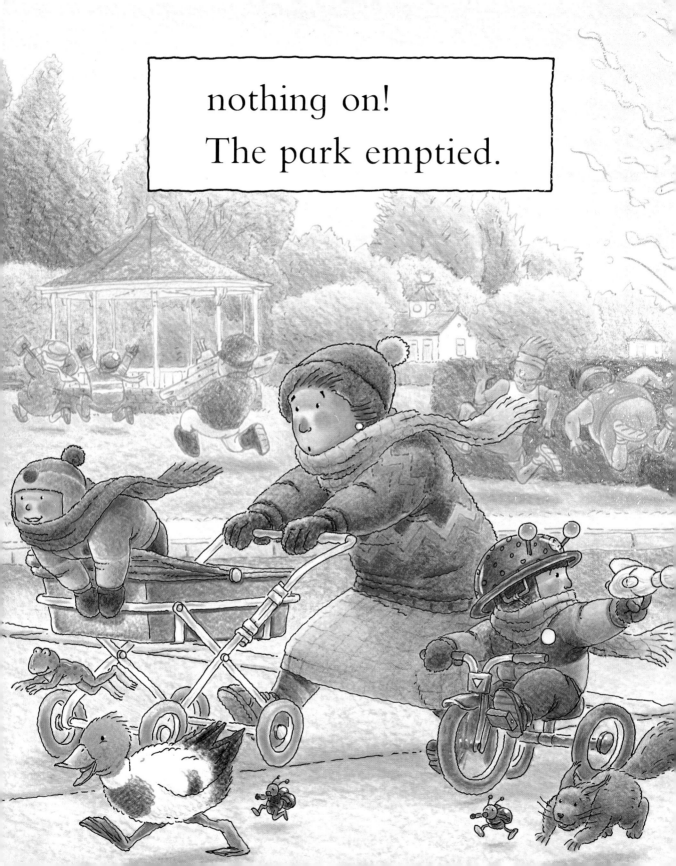

nothing on!
The park emptied.

Sidney laughed.
And went home.

"I'm still bored," said Sidney.
"And being bored is boring.
Time for more frightening."

So he went to a school,

looked through a window and…

made a monstrously rude noise!
All the children ran out…

except for Millie.

Sidney poked his tongue out at her.
Millie smiled.

Sidney shouted "BOO!" at her.
Millie giggled.

Sidney ran round with nothing on.
Millie laughed.

Sidney made a monstrously
rude noise. Millie roared.

"This isn't right," said Sidney.
"You're meant to be frightened."

"I'm not frightened of you," said
Millie. "You're funny. Look!"
They smiled, they giggled,
they laughed, they roared.

And they went home.